Millions of Americans remember Dick and Jane (and Sally and Spot too!). The little stories with their simple vocabulary words and warmly rendered illustrations were a hallmark of American education in the 1950s and 1960s.

But the first Dick and Jane stories actually appeared much earlier—in the Scott Foresman Elson Basic Reader Pre-Primer, copyright 1930. These books featured short, upbeat, and highly readable stories for children. The pages were filled with colorful characters and large, easy-to-read Century Schoolbook typeface. There were fun adventures around every corner of Dick and Jane's world.

Generations of American children learned to read with Dick and Jane, and many still cherish the memory of reading the simple stories on their own. Today, Pearson Scott Foresman remains committed to helping all children learn to read—and love to read. As part of Pearson Education, the world's largest educational publisher, Pearson Scott Foresman is honored to reissue these classic Dick and Jane stories, with Grosset & Dunlap, a division of Penguin Young Readers Group. Reading has always been at the heart of everything we do, and we sincerely hope that reading is an important part of your life too.

Dick and Jane

Fun with Our Family

Dick and Jane® is a registered trademark of Addison-Wesley Educational Publishers, Inc. Text and illustrations from THE NEW GUESS WHO, copyright © 1965 by Scott, Foresman and Company, copyright renewed 1993; FUN WITH THE FAMILY, copyright © 1965 by Scott, Foresman and Company, copyright renewed 1993.

Published by Grosset & Dunlap, a division of Penguin Young Readers Group, 345 Hudson Street, New York, New York 10014. GROSSET & DUNLAP is a trademark of Penguin Group (USA) Inc. Printed in the U.S.A.

ISBN 0-448-43568-3   10 9 8 7 6 5 4 3 2 1

Dick
and
Jane
Fun with Our Family

GROSSET & DUNLAP • NEW YORK

# CONTENTS

Spot

Here, Spot.
Here, Spot.
Look here.

Jump, Spot!
Jump, jump.

Oh, Spot!

Jane

Jane said, "Look!
Look here, Dick."

Jane said, "Oh, oh!
Help! Help!"

Dick said, "Go, Jane.
Jump! Jump!
Jump, Jane!"

Jump, Sally

Sally said, "Look, Jane!
Look at me, Jane!"

Sally said, "Oh, oh!
Come here, Jane.
Come and help me.
Help! Help!"

Jane said, "Go, go!
Jump, Sally, jump!"

Father

Dick said, "Father! Father!
Look at me.
Here I go.
Come and get me."

Father said, "Run, Dick.
Here I come.
Run! Run!"

Father said, "No, Spot, no!
Look at Dick.
Get Dick.
Go and get Dick!"

Mother and Sally

Mother said, "Oh, Sally.
Come here and get Puff.
Run, Sally, run!"

Sally said, "No, Puff!
No, no!
You come here, Puff."

Sally said, "Oh, Mother!
Look at Puff.
Look at me.
Puff and I can help you."

Spot and Dick

Mother said, "Come here, Dick.
Can you jump?
Spot can jump.
Can you?"

Mother said, "No, Spot.
Not you! Not you!
Down, Spot, down!"

Dick said, "Down, Spot!
I can get that."

Here Is Dick

Father said, "Come here, Dick.
I want you.
You can help me."

Father said, "Dick! Dick!
Come here.
I want you to help me.
Come here and help!"

Jane said, "Oh, Father.
That is not Dick.
Here is Dick."

Jump Down

Sally said, "Look, Mother.
That is Puff.
Look at Puff run."

Mother said, "Oh, Sally.
That is not Puff.
Puff is here with me."

Sally said, "Puff! Puff!
Get down.
I want you to jump down.
I want you to run and play.
Jump down, Puff."

"Oh, Sally!" said Mother.

"Puff did jump down.

Come here, Sally.

Come here and play with Puff."

Find Sally and Tim

Mother said, "I want to find Sally.
And I want to find Tim.
I want to find Sally and Tim."

Sally said, "Run, Mother.
Find Tim and me."

Mother said, "Sally is down here.
Tim is with Sally.
I can find Sally and Tim."

"No, no, Mother," said Sally.
"You can not find me."

Mother said, "Here is Tim.
I did find Sally and Tim!"

Sally said, "Oh, no, Mother.
Tim is not with me.
Tim is with Father.
You did not find me."

Play Ball

Penny said, "I want to play.
I can get the ball."

Father said, "No, Penny.
You can not get the ball.
You go and play with Pam."

Penny said, "I can play ball.
I can get the ball."

"You can not!" said Mike.
"Go away, Penny, go away."

Penny said, "Look, Mike, look!
Look at the ball.
I did get the ball.
I did! I did! I did!"

Pam and Penny

Mike said, "Come here, Pam.
Come here, Penny.
Come and play with me."

"No, Mike," said Pam.
"Penny and I can not play.
We can not play with you."

"Look, Father, look!" said Mike.
"See Pam and Penny run away."

Father said, "Come here, Pam!
Come here, Penny!"

Mike said, "Pam! Penny!
You can not run away."

Penny said, "Oh, Mike.
We did not want to run away.
Look at Mother.
We want to help Mother."

Come and See

Mike said, "Come here.

Pam and I want you.

We want you to come and see."

Mother said, "Oh, Mike.
I can see Pam."

Father said, "Look at that!
Is that Pam?"

Mike said, "No, no!
That is not Pam.
That is Pam and Penny."

Get the Ball

Penny said, "Jump, Mike.
You can get the ball down."

Mike said, "Come with me, Pam.
I want you to help me.
We can get the ball down."

Pam said, "Oh, Mike.
I can not help you.
I can not get the ball down."

Pam said, "Look, Penny.
See that!
I did get the ball down!"

Mike said, "No, Pam.
You did not get the ball.
We did."

Find Mike

Penny said, "Oh, Mother.
Pam and I can not find Mike.
We want to play with Mike.
Can you find Mike?"

Mother said, "I can find Mike.
I can see Mike.
And Mike can see me."

Pam said, "I can not see Mike.
Mike is not here."

Mike said, "Penny! Pam!
Did you want me?"

Pam said, "Oh, Mother.
You did find Mike.
You did! You did!"

Dick

No, Spot!
No, no!

Help! Help!

Oh, Spot!

Sally

Dick said, "Come, Sally."

Sally said, "Oh, no, Dick.
No, no, no!"

Dick said, "Here, Spot.
Come here.
Come here, Spot."

Sally said, "Dick!
Here I come!
Here I come, Dick!"

Help Spot

"Oh, Jane," said Sally.
"Look here.
Help Spot!
Help Spot!"

"Here, Spot," said Jane.
"I want you.
Look here."

Sally said, "Oh, Jane!
You can help Spot.
You can!"

See Sally Help

Sally said, "Jump down, Dick!
Puff and I want to play.
We want to play with the ball.
Jump down and go away!"

Dick said, "Come here, Jane.
I want you.
Come and help me."

Sally said, "Oh, Jane!
See Dick and Spot!"

"Here, Dick," said Jane.
"I can help you."

Sally said, "I want to help.
Here I come."

Jane said, "Oh, Dick!
Look at Sally!"

Sally said, "Look at me!
See me help.
See me help Spot."

Mike and Penny

Mike said, "Here, Penny.
I want to help you.
Look at me.
I can help you."

Mike said, "Come here, Pam.
See me help Penny."

Pam said, "I want to help.
I want to help Penny."

Penny said, "Oh, Mike.
Look at Pam!
Oh, oh, oh!"

Look at That

Penny said, "Look, Mike.
I can help you."

"No, no, Penny!" said Mike.
"Go to Mother.
Go and help Mother."

"Here, Penny," said Mother.
"You can help Pam and me."

Penny said, "I want that!
Oh, Mother, I want that!"

Penny said, "Not that!
Not that, Mother.
I did not want that."

Can Pam Find Mike?

Pam said, "I see you, Penny.
I can find you.
Come with me.
Come and help me find Mike."

"Oh, Father," said Pam.
"Penny and I want to find Mike.
I can not find Mike.
Did Mike go away?"

"No, Pam," said Father.
"Mike did not go away.
You can find Mike."

Penny said, "Oh, oh!
See that!"

Father said, "Look, Pam.
Penny and I see Mike.
We see Mike.
Look, Pam, look!"

See Puff Play

Sally said, "Look here, Father.
Look at Puff.
See Puff play with the ball."

Dick said, "Oh, Sally!
I want that ball."

Sally said, "Father! Father!
Did you see Puff jump?
Oh, oh, oh!
Look at Dick!"

Find Tim

Sally said, "I want Tim.
Help me, Mother.
I can not find Tim."

Dick said, "Oh, Mother.
I can help Sally.
We can go and find Tim."

Dick said, "Jump down, Spot.
Sally and I can not play with you.
We want to find Tim.
Go away!
Run and find Tim."

Sally said, "Oh, look at that!"

Sally said, "Mother! Mother!
Come and get me.
Run, Mother, run!"

Dick said, "Look, Sally.
Here is Tim!
Spot did find Tim!"

Here Is the Ball

Dick said, "Run away, Puff.
Jane and I want to play here.
We want to play with the ball."

Jane said, "Get down, Puff.
Run and find Sally.
Go play with Sally and Tim."

Jane said, "Father! Father!
I can not get the ball down.
Can you help me, Father?
Can you jump and get the ball?"

Dick said, "Oh, Jane.
I can get the ball down."

Dick said, "Here, Jane.
Here is the ball."

Jane said, "Mother! Father!
Did you see that?
Did you see the ball come down?
Dick did that!"

Dick Helps Jane

Jane said, "Come here, Dick.
Will you help me with this?
I want to get this down.
Will you help me?"

Dick said, "I will help you.
I can get this down.
Look at me.
Down I go!
Down I go now!"

Dick said, "Oh, Jane!
This is not funny."

Jane said, "That is funny.
Now I will have to help you."

Puff Wants a Ride

Dick said, "Look at Puff.
Puff wants a ride."

Sally said, "No, no, Puff!
You can not ride in that car.
Go away, Puff.
I want Tim to ride now."

Sally said, "Oh, Puff!
See what you did!
Now the cars will not go.
Run away, Puff.
Run away!
I want Tim to have a ride."

Dick said, "See Puff go!
The cars will go now.
See Puff go with the cars."

Sally said, "Run, Puff, run!
Tim can have a funny ride now.
Tim can have a ride with you."

Father and Dick

Mother said, "Come, Sally.

I want you to go with Jane and me.

Jane is in the car.

Run and get in the car with Jane."

Dick said, "Oh, Mother!
I want to go with you."

Father said, "Come here, Dick.
You can help me with this.
You and I will see what we can do."

Father said, "Look here.
See this go up.
Now down it comes.
See me get it."

Dick said, "I can do that.
I want to do that now."

Dick said, "Look!
See this big one go up.
Now see me get it."

Father said, "Oh, Dick!
You did not get it.
Tim did."

The Big Red Book

Mike said, "Mother!
Did you see a red book?"

Mother said, "No, Mike."

Pam said, "I have a red book.
It is a funny one.
Is this what you want?"

"No, no," said Mike.
"That is not my book.
My book is not a funny one.
It is a big one with cars in it."

"Oh, Father," said Mike.
"Did you see my red book?
It is a big one with cars in it."

Father said, "No, Mike.
I did not see it."

Mike said, "Penny!
Do you have my big red book?"

"Penny!" said Mike.

"You do have my book.

Get up, Penny.

Up, up!

I want that big red book.

You can have two little ones."

Penny Works

Penny said, "Work, work, work!
Mother and Father work.
Mike works.
And I can not find Pam.
Who will play with me?"

Mother said, "Here, Penny.
Will you go to the car with this?
We can not play with you now.
But you can help with the work."

Penny said, "Oh, I want to work.
I will go to the car with this.
I like to work."

Penny said, "Oh, Pam!
Look in here.
Do you see what I see?
It is something we like."

Mother said, "Penny is not here.

Pam is not here.

Mike, will you find Pam and Penny?"

Mike said, "Look at this!

Who wants to see something funny?

Come and look at Penny and Pam."

Three Little Dogs

Pam said, "Is that a dog, Mother?
What a funny little dog!"

Mother said, "Penny! Mike!
Come and see two little dogs."

"Look!" said Penny.
"I see three little dogs.
Not two little dogs, but three!"

Pam said, "I like this one.
See what it can do.
Look at this little dog.
See what it will do for me."

Penny said, "Look at this little dog.
See what it will do for me.
I want this one."

Pam said, "Oh, this is fun.
I like the three little dogs.
I want a little dog."

Mike said, "Look at this!
I want this little dog, Father.
Will you get three little dogs for us?"

Father said, "Not three dogs!
We will look for one big dog.
But we can not get three dogs."

Who Will Jump?

"See what I have," said Mike.
"I want to do something with this.
I want to have a little fun."

Penny said, "Oh, Mike.

I can guess what you want.

You want me to jump.

But that is not fun for me.

I do not want to jump."

Mike said, "I want Pam to jump.

Come and help me find Pam."

"Oh, this is fun!" said Penny.
"Pam is in the house.
I want to see Pam jump."

"Come with me," said Mike.
"Come in the house with me.
You will see something funny."

Mike said, "Look, Penny.
Now you will see something funny.
You will see Pam jump.
One ... two ..."

"Three!" said Penny.
"One, two, three!
Pam did not jump.
But you did."

A Ride with Father

Pam said, "Father! Father!
Penny and I want to go with you.
We like to ride in the car."

Father said, "Who will find Mike?
I guess Mike will want to go with us."

"Here comes Mike!" said Pam.

Penny said, "Come for a ride, Mike.
Run, run!"

Father said, "Now we can go.
Jump in the car, you three."

Penny said, "What a little ride!
We want to go for a big ride.
This is not fun for us, Father."

Father said, "You will have fun.
But we can not go now.
I can not see."

"Now I can see," said Father.
"We will go for a big ride."

Pam said, "Not now, Father.
You can see.
But now Mike can not see."

Away We Go

Mike said, "Look here.
Away I go!"

Penny said, "See me!
I can go with Mike.
Away we go!"

Pam said, "Mother! Father!
See Penny and me.
We can go with Mike.
Away we go!"

"Look here," said Father.
"Look at Mother and me.
Here we come."

Pam said, "Away we go!
Mike and Penny and me.
Father and Mother.
Away we go!"